STEP INTO READING® will help your child get   The program offers
five steps to reading success. Each step includes f   tories and colorful art.
There are also Step into Reading Sticker Books, S   ıto Reading Math
Readers, Step into Reading   eaders, Step   Read   ı-In
Readers, and Step into   Boxed Se   a co   y
program with somethi   child.

Learning to Re   tep!

Ready to   ool–Kindergai
• big type an   rhyme and rhythm
For children who know the alphabet and are ea
begin reading.

Reading with Help   Preschool–Grade 1
• basic vocabulary • short sentences • simple stories
For children who recognize familiar wo   nd sound out
          rds with help.

our Own   G
          cters • easy-t
For childr   who are ready

Paragraphs
          ıging vocabulary • s
          newly independent re
with confidence.

Ready for Chapters
• chapters • longer paragr
For children who want to   oks
but still like colorful pictures.

STEP INTO READING® is designed to give ever   essful
reading experience. The grade levels are only guides. Children can progress
through the steps at their own speed, developing confidence in their
reading, no matter what their grade.

Remember, a lifetime love of reading starts with a single step!

For Lucy Rae
—M.L.

Visit us on the Web!
StepIntoReading.com
www.randomhouse.com/kids

Educators and librarians, for a variety of teaching tools, visit us at
www.randomhouse.com/teachers

ISBN: 978-0-7364-2765-4 (trade)—ISBN: 978-0-7364-8091-8 (lib.bdg.)

Printed in China

DISNEY · PIXAR

Cars

GO, GO, GO!

By Melissa Lagonegro
Illustrated by Ron Cohee, Art Mawhinney,
and the Disney Storybook Artists

Random House 🏠 New York

Thanks, God!

Everyone is on the go in Radiator Springs!

5

Lightning is
a race car.
He drives fast.

Mater is a tow truck.
He pulls cars
out of trouble.

Fillmore is a van.

He is green.

He makes fuel.

Mack is a trailer truck.

He carries Lightning.

Al Oft is a blimp.

He floats

in the sky.

Red is a fire truck.

He has a water hose.

Tractors have big wheels.

They tip over easily.

Sheriff is a police car.
He has a red light
and a siren.

Guido is a forklift.

He carries tires.

The helicopter flies
in the air.
Its blades spin
around and around!

Sarge is a 4x4.

He rides

over rocks.

Frank is a combine.

He cuts grain.

The train rides

on a track.

Bulldozers are big
and strong.

Go, go, go!